Jenny's
Baby Brother

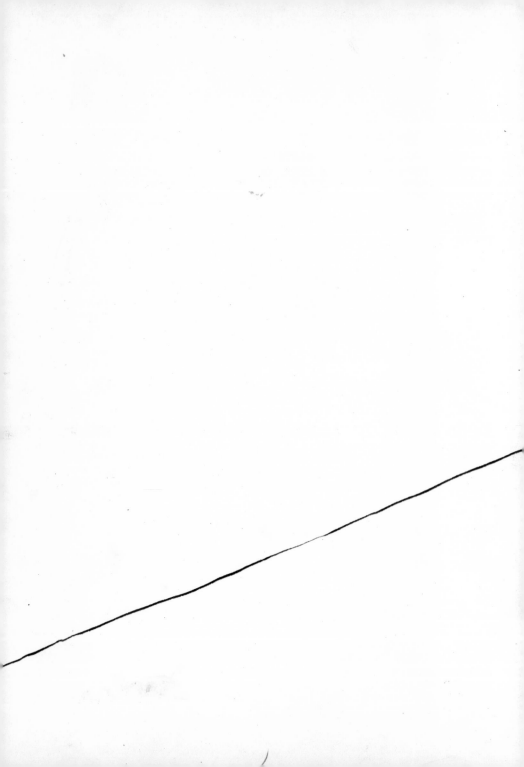

JE

c.1

First American Edition
Originally published in 1981 by William Collins Pty Ltd, Sydney
Text Copyright © 1981 by Peter Smith
Illustrations Copyright © 1981 by Bob Graham
All rights reserved.
Published in 1984 by The Viking Press
40 West 23rd Street, New York, N.Y. 10010
Published simultaneously in Canada by
Penguin Books Canada Limited
Printed in Hong Kong
1 2 3 4 5 88 87 86 85 84

Library of Congress Cataloging in Publication Data
Smith, Peter, 1943–   Jenny's baby brother.
   Summary: At first, Jenny is unhappy because her baby brother is too
young to play with, but soon he joins in the fun.
   [1. Brothers and sisters — Fiction.   2. Babies —
Fiction]   I. Graham, Bob, ill.   II. Title.
PZ7.S65756Je   1984   [E]   83-23350   ISBN 0-670-40636-8

Jenny's
Baby Brother

PETER SMITH
Illustrations by BOB GRAHAM

THE VIKING PRESS
New York

4858 59

For Naomi

Jenny had a baby brother and she didn't like him much. He was round and dimpled and crawled around the floor most of the time.

He was alright if you just wanted something soft to prod or cuddle but he wasn't much fun.

He was good at gurgling and sleeping and
making a mess when he had his dinner. But
there wasn't much you could really do with him.

"When is he going to be old enough to play with?" Jenny asked her mother.

But her mother just poked another spoonful of porridge into her brother's mouth and said, "I think he's lovely just as he is."

So Jenny played around on her own.
Swinging from a tree,
skipping up to two hundred,

and throwing a ball against the wall.

Baby brother watched her from his frilly pink
cradle, and Jenny poked out her tongue at him.
He smiled and blew bubbles of spit.

She showed off to him, even though he didn't
know what was going on. She did handstands
and cartwheels and raced up to where he lay
snoozing to wake him with ugly faces and loud
shrieks.

She brought her school friends to visit and
they all thought he was gorgeous, so she didn't
bring them again.

"I wish he would stay like this forever," said her Dad, and Jenny scowled into her peaches and ice cream. Her brother was covered in food, he didn't seem to be getting any better.

Then one magic day, Jenny's brother did
something interesting.

He was sitting at the table opposite her and
suddenly he picked up his spoon, which was
filled with runny custard.

He looked across the table, paused, and then
flicked the loaded spoonful straight into Jenny's
eye.

"Waaaaagh!" she said, but really she thought it
was a terrific shot.

A week later she came home from school and
passed Pete in the hall. He put out a chubby
foot and tripped her up.

"Good for you, Pete!" she said, dabbing at a
bleeding lip.

Suddenly her fat little brother didn't seem to be lolling around so much. He started to follow her everywhere and she had to shut the door of her room to keep him out.

She found him in the garden one day and he
was trying to throw the ball against the wall.
She showed him how to do it.

He tried to do a somersault and hurt himself,
so she patted his plump cheeks until he gurgled
again.

She brought her friends around and felt a bit
proud when they said he was gorgeous.

When she played in the garden her baby brother
tried to join in, in his clumsy bumbling way, and
she didn't mind any longer.

He was getting to be more fun every day. He
even did some things that she wasn't allowed to
do. Like ripping up flowers and digging holes
in the lawn.

One day her Mum said to her, "Aren't you going
to play with your friends today?"

"No," replied Jenny, "I'm going out in the garden to play with my baby brother.

And she rolled him all the way down the lawn.

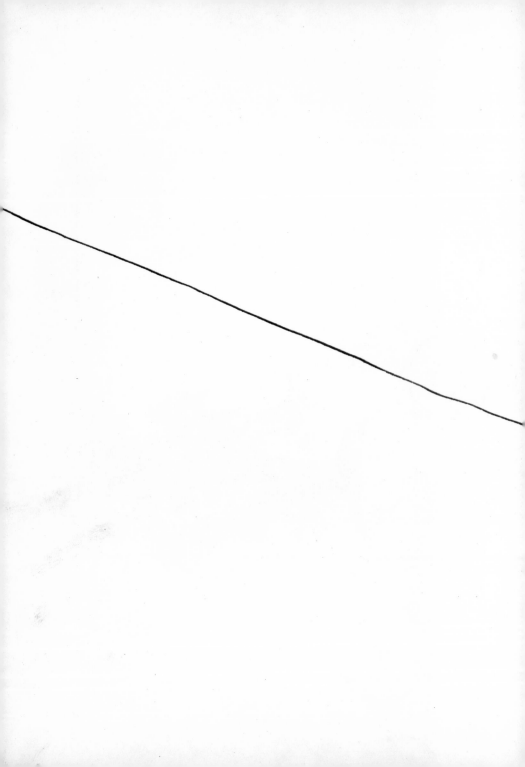